When Night Became Day

Jules Miller

Sky Pony Press
New York

Once upon a different time,
way up in the darkest part of the sky,
the moon was in a mood.

He was bored of the same old routine.
Nothing much ever happened.

For Nic, Rhianna, and Louis;
you are my sunshine.

The Miller Family

Copyright © 2014 by Jules Miller

Sky Pony Press books may be purchased in bulk at special discounts for sales promotion, corporate gifts, fund-raising, or educational purposes. Special editions can also be created to specifications. For details, contact the Special Sales Department, Sky Pony Press, 307 West 36th Street, 11th Floor, New York, NY 10018 or info@skyhorsepublishing.com.

Sky Pony® is a registered trademark of Skyhorse Publishing, Inc.®, a Delaware corporation.

Visit our website at www.skyponypress.com.

10 9 8 7 6 5 4 3 2 1

Manufactured in China, October 2014
This product conforms to CPSIA 2008

Library of Congress Cataloging-in-Publication Data
Miller, Jules, author, illustrator.
When night became day / by Jules Miller.
pages cm
ISBN 978-1-62914-632-4 (hardback)
[1. Moon--Fiction. 2. Sun--Fiction. 3. Night--Fiction. 4. Day--Fiction.] I. Title.
PZ7.1.M58Wh 2015
[E]--dc23
2014023921

Cover design by Danielle Ceccolini
Cover illustration credit Jules Miller

Ebook ISBN: 978-1-63220-233-8

Bored

Then during one very dull night,
the moon had a rather bright idea.

He decided to go and
tell his friend the sun.

The moon found the sun
in the lightest blue part of the sky,
where he was busy chasing away a few gray clouds.

Crack of Dawn

Daybreak Dew

Snoozy Sunrise

Midday Melt

Jolly Afternoon

Sunset Sparkle

Twilight Twirl

Night Night Navy

Midnight Shadow

"I want to swap jobs with you!" announced the moon excitedly. "I'm fed up with being up all night with only a bunch of boring stars for company."

"Well," replied the sun, "my job is no easier, you know, rising at the crack of dawn — it's very hot work, shining all day."

The sun considered the idea while the moon waited patiently. "Okay, Moon, let's do it — let's swap jobs!" said the sun, suddenly feeling rather excited.

So as dawn broke that summer morning...

the sun puffed and fluffed

100% CLOUD
HAND WASH ONLY
DRIP DRY

his favorite cloud pillow...

and went back to bed.

Meanwhile...

the moon got right to work on turning night into day.

He squeezed...

...and he wheezed

...and he squeezed some more.

But, there was just one problem:
no matter how hard the moon shone,
he was just not as shiny as the sun.

Consequently,
down on earth it was suddenly much too dark for daytime,
which made everybody think that it was still night.

Nobody could see whether they were coming or going!

Things were really no better in the town.

It was chaos.

Milkmen cried over spilt milk,

and in the restaurants

too many cooks spoiled the broth.

At the seashore, the tide was out
when it should have been in.

Very soon nothing was as it should be, and everything that should be, wasn't.
The moon had shone beautifully all day, but it was still really rather dark.

The moon decided to talk to the sun again.

"How was your day?"
asked the sun, surprised to see his
friend looking so exhausted.

"Not nearly as much fun
as I thought it would be,"
replied the moon, feeling like a failure.
"In fact, it's all a bit of a mess down there."

Daily Sunshine

BO PEEP
Sheep lost as dark day
disaster continues

World dips into twilight as Moon replaces Sun

Bo Peep this afternoon

"Sheep could be anywhere by now," expert Professor Wool tells our reporter, before explaining that Little Bo Peep's sheep often "went into hiding, but this time the low light is on their side."

Sheep - last seen yesterday

The travel news magazine
Voyage

Owl and Pussycat Exclusive:
The Trip's off!
How the sudden darkness "wrecked" their travel plans...

The Dawn Chorus
Latest breaking news from the bird community

FREE

NO SUN - NO SONG

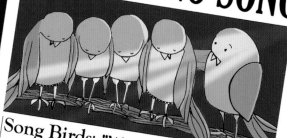

Song Birds: "We won't be singing in the dark, we'll just go on strike."

A little bird has told us that, because of the recent lack of sunlight, our song birds are not able to sing. "They need the sun to make them feel like singing," he said.

The sun, who'd been daydreaming about his quiet night ahead, told the moon not to worry.

"I'll figure it out," he said confidently and, turning himself up to "high heat," he set off.

Moments later,
the sun was
beaming!

"This is the life," he said to himself while admiring the quiet, sleepy earth below.

But before long, everyone who should have been asleep woke up!
It was the middle of the night,
but it was just too hot to sleep.

"Hmm," muttered the sun, feeling rather annoyed. "I'll show them!"
And with that, he took a deep, fiery breath and shone even brighter.

NIGHTS ARE
FOR SLEEPS
NOT TWEETS!

Just then, a couple of mischievous gray clouds passed by the sun.

"Not so popular now, are you?"
they taunted.

The sun, feeling quite embarrassed, had had enough. Perhaps this wasn't such a good idea after all.

SUN— YOU'RE A BIRD BRAIN

The sun decided
to find the moon
and tell him it just
wasn't working out.

"I think we both may have

learned a valuable lesson,"

began the sun in his warmest voice.

"While we can't always be good at everything,

everyone's good at something."

The moon —
suddenly feeling rather sleepy
— agreed with the sun.
In fact, he actually preferred
the navy blue night sky.
He even missed the stars!

Night Night Navy

Taller!! Tallest!!!
The Tallest Flower
Prize Grower

Science Buff

Ball Champ

PICK YOUR OWN DAISIES

Important Notice:
Cloud Spotters, Kite Flyers,
Bird Watchers, Sky Divers,
Picnic Eaters, Dog Walkers,
City Dwellers, Tree Huggers,
Picture Painters, Daisy Pickers,
Hill Climbers, Remote Controllers...

. . . if during the daytime you do happen to see the moon,
and it's past his bedtime, it may just be that he's taking a quick
peek at our world when he thinks we're not looking.